THE STUPIDS HAVE A BALL

TRA LA

HARRY ALLARD · JAMES MARSHALL

Houghton Mifflin Company Boston

Library of Congress Cataloging in Publication Data

Allard, Harry.
   The Stupids have a ball.

   SUMMARY: The Stupid family celebrates the children's
awful report cards by inviting their relatives to a
costume party.
   [1. Humorous stories.   2. Parties—Fiction]
I.   Marshall, James, 1942-   joint author.
II.   Title.
PZ7.A413Sq   [E]   77-27660

RNF   ISBN   0-395-26497-9
PAP   ISBN   0-395-36169-9

Printed in the United States of America

WOZ   20   19   18   17   16   15   14

For Eve Fréjaville and Adolph Garza
with love

Report card time had rolled around again.
Mr. and Mrs. Stupid could hardly wait for
Buster and Petunia to get home from school.

"Hooray!" cried Mr. Stupid. "This time Buster
and Petunia flunked *everything!*"
"And *that's* hard to do," said his wife.
The two Stupid kids beamed from ear to ear.
"This calls for a celebration!" declared Mr. Stupid.
"Why don't we have a costume ball and invite
all our relatives?" said Mrs. Stupid.
"You know how they all like to get dressed up."

The Stupids' wonderful cat, Xylophone, was
so excited her tail got stuck in her nose.

While Xylophone blew up party balloons,
Mr. and Mrs. Stupid and the Stupids' wonderful
dog, Kitty, wrote out the invitations.
"Oh dear," said Mrs. Stupid. "I don't know how
to spell Cousin Dottie Stupid's last name."
"That's a tough one all right," said her husband.

That afternoon, Kitty and Xylophone made
punch in the kitchen.
"Their punch is always so tasty," whispered
Mrs. Stupid. "I wonder what the secret
ingredients are?"
The two Stupid kids smacked their lips.

"Time to put on our costumes!" Mrs. Stupid called out.

When Petunia saw her father's costume, she squealed with delight.

"I'm General George Washing Machine," said Mr. Stupid.

"I can see that, Daddy," said Petunia.

"Gosh!" cried Buster. "My Rudolf Rat costume is missing!"

"Never mind," said his mother, who was wearing some beautiful spaghetti. "You can always make up your own outfit."

A loud quacking was heard in the yard.
"That must be Cousin Dottie Stupid,"
said Mrs. Stupid. "She's the only one
in the family who drives a duck."
Cousin Dottie was always the first to arrive
at parties.
"This duck really *moves*," said Cousin Dottie.

Soon other members of the Stupid family began arriving.

"My, my," said Mr. Stupid. "I've never
seen so many Stupids together in one room."
"There's Uncle Angus MacStupid,"
said Mrs. Stupid.
"Which one is he?" said her husband.

"Oh look!" squealed Petunia. "It's
Grandfather Stupid!"
Grandfather Stupid came down the chimney.
He was dressed as the Easter Bunny.
"Ho, ho, ho," he said.

The Stupids' guests were all enjoying
themselves immensely.
And everyone thought little Ichabod Stupid
was very cute when he dangled his toes
in the punch.

But Grandfather Stupid was having
the most fun of all.
"You sure can polka, Dot," he said.

When the ball was over and the last guest
was leaving, Mr. Stupid turned to his wife.
"Did you notice that we were the only ones
wearing costumes?" he said. "The other
Stupids came in their everyday clothes."
"Oh dear," said Mrs. Stupid. "I forgot
to mention that it would be a *costume* ball."
"Never mind," said Buster. "We all had
a wonderful time, General."
"We always do," said Mr. Stupid, closing
the door.